THE
Marvellous
MOON
MAP

For Luca
T.H.

For Katie,
Ben & George
D.L.

THE Marvellous MOON MAP

Teresa Heapy • David Litchfield

RED FOX

Mouse and Bear lived in a little, dark house in the big, black Woods, and today Mouse wanted to find the Moon.

"I'm off to the Moon, Bear!" said Mouse. "On my own!
I'm making a Moon Map to show me the way."
"Mouse," said Bear, "why don't you sit down? I'll help you
pack up . . . then we'll set off together!"

"No, Bear," said Mouse, firmly. "I don't need your help – I'm the Moon Map Inventor! I'll go on my own."

Mouse worked on his Moon Map.

He planned,
and he thought,

he watched,
and he wrote.

He read, and he tweaked
and he measured and drew.

It was a magnificent, mighty, most marvellous Moon Map.

"Right then," said Bear, "we'll need
torches and jumpers, and gloves to keep warm,
and a hot flask of tea . . ."
"All I need is my Moon Map!" said Mouse.
"Are you *sure*?" murmured Bear.
"Oh yes, Bear!" said Mouse. "I know the way now!
I'll be back before tea!"

So Mouse set off,
on his own,
on his way to the Moon.

He looked at his Moon Map,
he tunnelled,
he climbed,

and he clambered
up into the Woods.

Now, things moved in the Woods.
Things fluttered, and scraped,
and rustled, and sighed there . . .

"Moon Map, show me the way,"
whispered Mouse – but all
he saw was the Dark.

And then came

a CRUNCH,

a SNAP and

a WHISPER.

Eyes flashed in the shadows
and bent towards Mouse.
"I can go on my own,"
    breathed Mouse,
        "on my own, on my own . . ."

When out came . . .

Bear!
"Hello, Mouse," he said.
"Need a hand?"

Mouse stumbled. "No, Bear, I don't need your help!
But it's so very dark – I can't see my Moon Map!"

"I know, Mouse," said Bear. "But I've got you,
and you've got me – so we'll be all right."

So Mouse felt his way, and Bear followed Mouse,
and they crept through the blackness and out of the Woods.
And there was the fat Moon, trailing milk in the water . . .

a long glitter of water,
swept out
before
them.

Mouse stopped. "Bear, look at my Moon Map!
We've got to go over – but it's too far to swim!"

"I know, Mouse," said Bear. "But I've got you,
and you've got me – so we'll be all right."

Bear looked at the Moon Map.
He looked very closely.
Then he folded it up.

Bear bent it in triangles, and pressed down the edges.
He tweaked and he tucked and he lifted . . .

. . . and opened.

He stroked,
and he smoothed,
and he flattened . . .

until Mouse's
Moon Map
was a little,
fat square.

"Bear, what have you
done?" said Mouse.
"Now we really are lost!"

"PULL, Mouse!"
said Bear.

"PULL!!"

So Mouse
pulled,

and Bear
pulled . . .

and the square of Map
opened,

grumbled,
and
grew,
and there was . . .

a boat!
Just right for two.

"Come on, quick, jump in!" said Bear.

For all of a sudden,
a storm and a wind were
above and around them,
shaking and spinning
and swirling the boat.

Mouse shivered. "Bear, we can't do it!
The waves are too high, and the boat is too small!"

"I know, Mouse," said Bear. "But I've got you,
and you've got me – so we'll be all right."

All through the night they
held tight to each other,
through the wild
and the wet
and the whirl of
the storm.

And, at last, the wind dropped.
It left them. But so did . . .

"The Moon! Bear, it's going!"
said Mouse. "The light's disappearing –
my Moon Map was all wrong!"
"No – look, Mouse," said Bear.
"Your marvellous Map took us here . . ."

"...to the Sun."

The Sun stroked the air with fingers of warmth,
and the sky glowed in pink, purple, orange and gold.
It tickled their ears and brushed warmth on their necks.
It stretched out their arms and put breath
in their tummies.

"Bear, shall we go home now?" said Mouse.
"Oh yes, Mouse," said Bear.
"But do you know the way back?
We don't have your Moon Map."

"I don't know, Bear," said Mouse. "But I've got you,
and you've got me – so we'll be all right."

The End

HOW TO MAKE

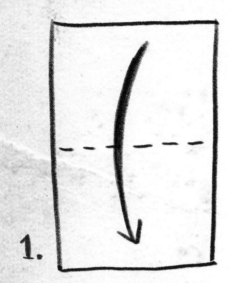

1. Colour in both sides of a piece of A4 paper with your favourite wax crayons (this will make it waterproof). Then fold it in half to create a rectangle.

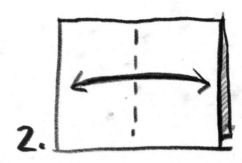

2. Fold this smaller rectangle in half again and unfold it, so that there is a fold line running through the centre of the folded paper.

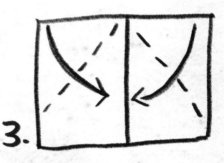

3. Fold the two top corners down to the centre fold.

4. Take one of the bottom rectangle strips and fold it upwards, partly covering the triangle.

5. Fold the overlapping corners backwards (creating two mini triangles on the other side).

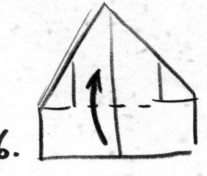

6. Turn over your paper and repeat steps 4 and 5 on the other side.

A PAPER BOAT
(DRAWN BY BEAR)

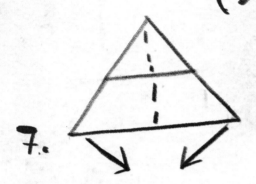

7.

You should now have a 'hat' shape. Put your thumbs inside the 'hat' and, holding the two sides, pull your hands together, closing your paper so that it flattens into a square shape.

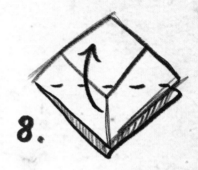

8.

Fold the bottom corner of your square upwards so that you are left with a triangle shape. Do the same on the other side.

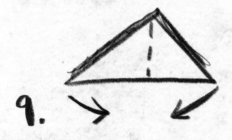

9.

As with step 7, put your thumbs in the corners and close them together, bringing the paper with you. You will end up with a little fat square.

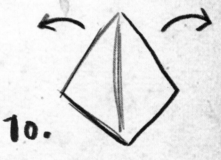

10.

Take the two upper corners of your square and stretch them out. You should now have a paper boat.

FINISHED
x

RED FOX

UK | USA | Canada | Ireland | Australia | India | New Zealand | South Africa

Red Fox is part of the Penguin Random House group of companies
whose addresses can be found at global.penguinrandomhouse.com.

www.penguin.co.uk   www.puffin.co.uk   www.ladybird.co.uk

Penguin
Random House
UK

First published 2017
001

Printed in China
A CIP catalogue record for this book is available from the British Library

ISBN: 978–1–782–95666–2

All correspondence to:
Red Fox, Penguin Random House Children's,
80 Strand, London WC2R 0RL

MIX
Paper from
responsible sources
FSC® C018179
FSC
www.fsc.org